A Plate of Christmas Cookies

By USA Today Bestselling Author

Dani Haviland

Copyright

Book Description

The day after the attack on Pearl Harbor, Jake enlists in the Marines. Separated from his sweetheart by duty and deception, he meets Mary again thirty-five years later and sparks fly.

Will the reunited couple shine or will his children turn their reignited romance to ash?

Praise and Awards

Chapter 1: On the Eve of War

December 6, 1941
Bisbee, Arizona

"Do we have any of that fancy red sugar?" Jake asked.

Mary sneaked up behind him and tiptoed to kiss him on the neck. "What's the matter? Aren't I sweet enough?"

He turned to face her, holding her with his elbows as he clutched a doughy spoon in each hand "Who taught you how to do that?" he asked, wrinkling his brow with the tease.

"You did," she said, then gave him a quick chaste kiss, hoping her mother didn't sneak in to check on them. "But my parents are in the other room listening to the Grand Ole Opry. I swear, I think they'd move to Nashville if they couldn't listen to it on the radio."

"I wouldn't let them," Jake said.

"Why?"

"Well, because they'd be taking you and I don't want you to leave."

"There's a way around that, you know," Mary said, smiling as she walked her fingers up his arm to his shoulder.

"Huh?"

"We could, you know..." Mary held up her left hand and wiggled her ring finger.

"What? Oh, you mean get married?"

"Yes! Yes, I'll marry you," Mary screeched in a restrained squeal. "But we can't tell anyone yet. I mean, we still have to graduate. That's not until June and that's..." She counted on her fingers, but Jake answered first.

"Six months away," he said absently, his mouth sagging from his initial smile to a frown, then back to a weak grimace.

"But I thought we wanted to be together forever," Mary pouted.

"We do. I do. It's just I didn't think it would be so soon. I have to find a career. I'd like to find a house, too. And a better car. That jalopy of mine is fun, but it isn't exactly a family wagon."

Mary blushed and looked down at her hands, rubbing them over each other nervously. "A family? You mean like children? Making babies?"

"Well," Jake said, sniffing back his hesitancy at the delicate subject, "that's usually how you get children. I mean, I guess we could adopt..." He looked down at her and grinned.

"Oh, no, no. I'd like to do it the other way. I mean, I'd like to have your child."

"Well, one thing's for certain. We have to be married first. So, Mary Decker," Jake got down on one knee, "this isn't how I planned to do this, but will you marry me?"

Mary grabbed the spoons out of his hands, noisily dropped them in the bowl of cookie dough, and tugged him to standing. "Yes! Yes! Yes, I'll marry you!"

"Shush," Jake whispered. "They might hear you. I don't think your folks would ever let me in the house again if they knew I'd asked you to marry me before we were eighteen. They'd think I was some sort of masher."

"Oops!" Mary put her hand over her mouth. "You're right. Sorry. Let's just keep it between the two of us for now. Well, except I'll have to tell Linda, for sure. I mean, what else are best friends for if not to share our deepest secrets?"

"How are those cookies coming along?" Mary's father called out from the living room.

Mary giggled. "Just give us a little bit more time. We're getting ready to put them in the oven now."

Papa stuck his head in the doorway. "Funny, it doesn't look like it." He laughed. "Just make sure there are enough for the Dear Santa Dance and me, too." He patted his ample belly. "Only so many are for the jolly old man himself; the rest are mine. Ah, Christmas – my favorite time of year."

"Papa, any time of year that includes sweet foods is your favorite time of year."

"True, but," he looked up at the clock, "the party starts in three hours. Remember, the cookies have to cool before you can frost them. Cookie exchanges aren't much fun without cookies."

Mary held up the bowl of sugar she'd colored red. "Drop cookies with sprinkles and a few strawberry-jam thumbprint cookies. I've never heard complaints before."

"Works for me. Oh, and Jake, you might want to clean up before you go. You look like you've been crawling through a flour mill."

Jake looked down and quickly brushed away the powdery traces of being on one knee. "Thank you, sir. We'll have everything ready."

"It's back on!" Mary's mother called out.

"Be right there," Papa replied, then turned to the two teenagers. "I was joking – sort of – about the extras. I want a few plates for our after-church get-together tomorrow. Hope you come, Jake."

"Yes, sir. I'll be there."

***

"Wow. I think the whole town showed up," Jake said, looking out across the basketball court. Teens and adults were dancing at one end, Santa sat in one corner with nearly a dozen children, and a table laden with colorfully wrapped parcels of cookies took up the other. "I thought only kids and moms would show up."

"Well, Santa *was* an attraction," Mary said, holding tight onto his arm, "but as soon as they added Dance to the theme, every high school kid from Douglas to Bisbee wanted to come. All this news about the war in Europe is depressing. Everyone's ready to have fun."

"Plus, there are the cookies. Do you see how many dads showed up? Your idea of auctioning them with all the proceeds going to Defense Bonds was great," Jake said, pulling her shoulder close in a hug. "Now people can either bid on the cookies or the wish. Highest earning wish will come true. I wonder which one will get the most?"

"Don't you want to know what wish I put on my plate?" Mary asked coyly.

"I thought you already got your wish," Jake whispered. "You got me to ask you to marry you."

Mary playfully punched his shoulder. "Rat. No, not that. And I didn't trick you."

Jake shrugged and grinned.

"I didn't!"

4

"Maybe not. I mean, I was already going to ask you, but I wanted to take you out to a nice restaurant with candlelight and flowers to do it. I had to wait until roses came in season, though."

"Jake, I would have said yes if you'd handed me a crayon drawing of flower."

He chuckled. "Yes, I guess you would have. As it was, I was empty-handed. I can't say I regret it, though."

"Ladies and gentlemen," the announcer called through a cheerleader's megaphone. "Last chance to see Santa Claus. He'll be here for ten more minutes, then has to hurry back to his workshop. So, hurry on over. At seven o'clock sharp, we're starting the auction. Bring your dollars and help support Defense Bonds. We hope to be out of here by eight so Mom can get the kids to bed."

Jake waited until the announcement was over, then leaned in and asked, "What did you wish for?"

Mary stuck her bottom lip out and remained mute.

"If you don't tell me, I'm gonna tickle you until you do..."

A smile tried to sneak in, but she bit it back. "No, you won't."

"Oh, yes I will. I don't care who's around." Turning to her, he reached for her ribs.

"Jake!" she squealed.

He reached up both hands in surrender and said, "I didn't do anything," then realized with all the ambient noise, no one had heard her.

"Sorry," she said. "Ask me to dance and I'll tell you."

"Mary, may I have the pleasure of this dance?" he asked, winking in mischief.

She put her hand on his shoulder and leaned close, comforted by his hand on her waist. "I wished for peace," she whispered.

"Amen to that. That one should get the highest bid."

Ten minutes later, the mayor was back on his megaphone, calling the bidders to the table. "Thanks for coming, everyone. I know you're waiting to get your chance to bid. All the money earned goes to a great cause: Defense Bonds. The world is in a rough place right now. Let's help the government be prepared. Dig deep. The missus doesn't need a vacuum cleaner this Christmas. Just buy her a new broom and dustpan and a bond or two."

The mayor lifted a fancy red plate wrapped in cellophane. "Okay, I'm starting from the right of the table tonight. No order, so don't accuse me of playing favorites," he said and smiled at his wife. "Now, the tag on this one says, 'My wish is for peace.' Now isn't that wonderful?"

The audience clapped and cheered.

"Is that one yours?" Jake whispered.

Mary shook her head and frowned. Someone else had the same idea.

The bidding started, ending at ninety-five cents. "Now, that's a great price. Let's see what this wish is for." He opened the folded-over paper taped to the plate. "This one is for peace, too. Now, let's see if we can beat the last one's bid."

After the third platter of cookies shared the same wish, someone called out, "Let's just bid on the cookies. Tell us what kind they are."

The mayor shrugged, lifted another plate, and looked through the cellophane. "This looks like jam thumbprint cookies and maybe sugar cookies with red sugar sprinkles."

"They're snickerdoodles," Jake called out. "And they're delicious."

"Yes, they are," Mary's father, still dressed in his Santa suit, hollered. He patted his ample tummy. "Just don't eat too many."

The crowd laughed, but bid heartily, her plate earning two dollars and fifty cents.

As they were leaving, Mary pulled Jake aside. "I made this one just for you. Mama said she'd like the plate back, though." She handed him a decorated Christmas plate wrapped in clear cellophane and an elaborate red bow. On it was a handmade tag with his name.

"My wish is for us to be together forever. Love, Mary," he read. Jake looked around, made sure no one was near, then kissed her gently. He pulled back. "That was for the cookies. This one's for the note." He wrapped his arms around her and lifted her a foot of the ground so they were at the same height. He kissed her deeply, daring to open his mouth and explore hers.

"Um!" she squeaked.

"Did I go too far?" he asked.

"No, I mean, someone might see us. Besides, if we're going to have children together, we'll have to do a lot more than that," she said, feeling her blush rise.

"But not until we're married," he reminded her.

She jumped up, grabbing him around his neck. "Until then, do that again. I'll try not to squeal."

***

"Glad you could make it, Jake," Mary's dad said.

"Thanks for inviting me, Mr. Decker. It was a nice service."

"Yes, and the spread looks great, too. Last night, I didn't think I could eat another cookie. Now look at them, each one calling my name." He picked up a napkin and started loading it up. "Decisions, decisions."

"Hey, everyone! Come over and listen," Pastor Green announced, rolling in the big radio from his office. He plugged it in and waited for it to warm up. "You're not gonna believe this."

"To repeat, the Japanese have invaded Pearl Harbor. Extensive damage..."

Everyone listened to the report, women sniffing, men snorting or saying, 'I knew something like this was gonna happen.' No one was as stunned as Jake.

Jake was still in school and only seventeen, but as soon as he graduated, he'd be drafted into the army.

"I'm enlisting in the Marines," he said to no one in particular.

"You're what?" Mary asked.

Jake looked at her and repeated, "I'm enlisting in the Marines. I'm pretty sure the recruiting station is closed today, but I'll be there first thing in the morning. I know we had plans..." He saw her father staring at him, wide-eyed at the declaration. "I'll be back when it's over. They need all the help they can get. What kind of man would I be if I didn't help my country?"

"Can I change my Christmas wish to you coming home safe?" Mary asked, tears welling in her eyes.

8

Jake nodded. "Yes, I'd like that. Now, I think I'd better go and tell my mother. She'll need to know. Looks like my baby brother is going to be the man of the house now."

Mr. Decker clapped a hand on Jake's back. "We'll watch out for her, too. I know it's been tough, you losing your dad last year, but she's part of the community. Thanks for volunteering, son."

"My honor, duty, and privilege, sir."

Chapter 2: 1945

February 17, 1945

"Okay, men," the sergeant said. "Listen up. We're landing on that big ugly gray pork chop – Iwo Jima – tomorrow. Bottom line, we're to take Mount Suribachi to keep the enemy from using it as a lookout. If you have letters to write, this might be your last chance at pen and paper for a while."

"Or ever," someone in the back of the group said under his breath, loud enough to be heard but not discovered as the source.

"Yes, it's doubtful we'll all make it out alive. But we're the 2nd Battalion, 28th Marine Regiment, 5th Marine Division, toughest sons of bitches in the world. Oorah!"

"Oorah!" the men echoed.

"Use the next sixty minutes however you want...except fighting with each other. Save that energy for the enemy. Dismissed."

Jake joined the others, grabbing a few fresh sheets of paper from the stack provided on the table.

"Are you writing to your gal again?" Scooter asked.

"You'd be sending letters to your girl, too," Jake said, then added, "if you had one."

The radioman threw an empty K ration can at Jake, but he'd expected it and ducked.

"She's moved on," Scooter said. "Betcha five bucks she'll send you a Dear John letter before this is over."

"No, not Mary. She's wanted to marry me since sixth grade, I think. I'm sure since we were sixteen. She's the first and only girl I've ever kissed."

Scooter shook his head and remained mute. Jake was going down in flames. Over three years of writing and only two ever answered. He'd have to let up on the teasing. And he certainly wasn't going to tell him that *no* woman ever waited. At least, none that he'd ever heard of. The boats, barracks, and bars were overflowing with stories of being spurned by 'the most perfect woman' who decided that the 4-F asthmatic accountant back home was worth more than sporadic letters from the 1-A soldier oversees, fighting with his life to keep his home and country safe.

***

February 23, 1945

"Don't tell me you're writing her another letter, Jake," Scooter teased.

Jake looked up and saw his best – and most irritating – friend standing above him, one eye bandaged, his hand wrapped in a muddy rag. "Nope, just trying to get rid of a few parts of me I don't need."

Scooter hobbled down the ditch to sit beside him. "What are you doing? Speak English."

Jake held up a pair of nail clippers. "Toenails. They've been killing me for ages. Finally found someone who had a pair I could borrow."

"Hmm. When you're done there, can I give them a swing? I

might be able to." Scooter held up his bandaged hand.

"You'd better get that looked at," Jake said. "You don't want to get it infected."

"Oh, it's bandaged nice and clean under this muddy cloth; it's just the over-bandage to keep me from hitting it on stuff. Lost my pinkie. Small sacrifice, I say."

Jake finished with the clippers then held them up for Scooter. When he reached for them with his bandaged hand, Jake pulled them back. "Nah, I'll do it. What are friends for? I'm sure you'd do the same for me."

"Let's hope that's the most you ever have to do for me. If the rumors are true, we're in Tojo's backyard now. Any day and we'll be done over here and home again." Scooter grinned. "And you can see Mary again."

Jake's gut clenched at the words. He'd known something was wrong for months now. Scooter's good-natured teasing about Mary was over. His kind words meant he was trying to soften the blow. After three years, it was obvious. She'd moved on. So much for true love.

***

February 27th, 1945
92nd Hospital, Luzon, Philippines

"It's just a scratch, Doc. I just want to get back to my unit."

"Nah. You're sticking around here until that fever goes down. The wound is fine. It's the malaria I'm worried about."

Jake leaned back in the bed, his weary body grateful for clean sheets and warm food. Even if the spirit was willing, he'd take the time to heal. Peace – and going home – were just weeks ahead.

"Jake Johnson?" the orderly called out.

He raised his hand and the teenage Filipino boy rushed over. "Jake Johnson with Second Battalion, Twenty-eighth?"

Jake nodded.

"Other man had these. He say he heard there was other Jake Johnson over here. These not his. He say he very sorry he read and keep them so long. He no get letters of his own."

Jake sat up straight despite his fever and fatigue, reaching for the tied bundle. There had to be two dozen envelopes, at least. His initial elation burned into a hard and hot coal of rage at someone else reading his precious letters from Mary, then he relaxed. At least they were here, and he was alive to read them.

"Oh, and for you. Other Jake Johnson say he buy you a beer, but since he cannot get one, this maybe to do until next time." The aide handed him a small bottle of Coca Cola. "Do you want me open for you?"

"No, not yet," he said, thinking of his queasy stomach. "Thanks."

"Oh, and he say many, many apologies. He told me say it until you get mad and tell me to leave."

Jake grinned. "How about we leave off the get mad part and I just tell you that's enough. *Bastanté*."

"*Bastanté?* You speak Spanish?"

"Yup. Halfway around the world, we have a common language. The Spanish settled the area where I came from, too. See you around,

13

Tigré. "

"Ah. *Adios, amigo. Adios* the young man said, leaving with a spring in his step as he punched the air, practicing his jabs like the Americans had shown him. "He thinks I a tiger. I like that name. World Champion Flyweight Tigré Macalino. I think I keep it."

Jake lay on his side and fanned the letters out, checking the postmarks. The other Jake had already sorted them by date. All were sent from Bisbee except the last one. It was from Las Vegas. Resisting the urge to start at the beginning, he opened the one from Nevada. That's all he'd need – to start reading and have a malarial attack before he found out why Mary was out of state.

Dear Jake,

I loved getting your letters, but they stopped. I didn't know if you were hurt or dead. Your mother said she hadn't received any notification, so we were hopeful. I don't know if you'll even get this. You never respond to any news I share or answered if you still care for me.

I never thought I'd be sending a Dear John letter, but I guess that's what this is. I was having a hard time dealing with Papa's death, trying to take care of Mama, and selling the house. Walter, the realtor from Douglas, was helping me. He helped me with all the packing, and once the house was sold, I didn't really know what to do or where to go. Mama was moving in with her sister and their family, but they didn't need me, too. Well, long story short, Walter asked me to marry him. He has asthma and had to move to somewhere that had cleaner air. The smelter smoke was too much for him. We married in

14

a small simple ceremony just before Mama left and we're now in Las Vegas. It's going to be a big town someday, he says.

I hope you're alive and not sad I got married. I also hope you find someone special.

Sincerely,

Mary Decker Hollingsworth

Tears were rolling down Jake's cheeks as he read the letter, pausing only long enough to wipe them on the pillow. "You were right, Scooter. They never wait."

Jake reached into the nightstand and took out his wallet, opening it to look at the slip of paper. 'My wish is for us to be together forever. Love, Mary.' He touched the edge of it, ready to take it out and crumple it and throw it in the trash. "Nope. It got me through a war. I'll save it as a token of endurance. A paper star of hope, not a bronze star of valor."

***

September 15, 1945

"Welcome home, soldiers!" the mayor announced. "We have a live band for your enjoyment tonight. We tried to get a big band, but Harry James was busy and couldn't make it. I guess if I were married to Betty Grable, I wouldn't want to go far from home, either."

The men in the audience cheered and whistled, and the women groaned and smacked them playfully on the shoulder. When they settled down, he continued, "Rather than not have a dance, a few of us old fogeys got together and learned some of your favorite hits. On a serious note, thank you, men, for sacrificing so much of your time and energies, fighting our enemies, and keeping America safe. In

appreciation, we put call outs in the newspaper and over the radio –
and even beat the tumbleweeds – to entice all the young single
women from Cochise County to attend our celebration. Now that
we're together, ladies and recently retired GI's, let's dance!"

"May I have this dance?"

Jake spun around, looking to see if someone had asked him.
There, standing just out of his peripheral vision, was Theresa
Oldman's little sister, Ellen. He recognized those big brown eyes, but
she was no longer the precocious tease who tossed walnuts at him
when he came to help her mother in the yard.

"It's me, Ellen," she said. "They told us we could ask you to
dance, that tonight it wasn't improper."

Jake shook his head, stunned. When she frowned and started to
turn away, he realized it looked like he was saying no. "Wait," he
said, his hand out. "I'm sorry. It's just you've changed so much. Yes,
I'd love to dance with you."

"So, you did recognize me?" she asked, accepting his hand.
"Otherwise, how would you know if I've changed?"

"You look all grown up now," he said, grinning, holding back the
smart aleck remarks he and his Marine buddies would have shared.

"It's been almost four years since you left. I'm a grown woman. I
even went to secretarial school. I'm going to get a job pretty soon. I
don't need to have a husband."

"Whoa," Jake said, his feet stilling. "What brought that on?"

Ellen took the lead in dancing, whispering, "Move. They're
staring at us."

The two started up again to the sometimes out of sync strains of

'Sentimental Journey.' "What did you mean by that? I didn't ask you to marry me," Jake said softly, his arms tingling with the newfound attraction.

"Sorry. Everywhere I go now, there's pressure to find a GI, get married, and make him grateful for the time and sacrifices he made. You know, thank him. Not me. When I marry, it's going to be for love. In the meantime, I'll get a job and earn my way in the world."

"What about children?" Jake asked.

"Well, I'd have to be married first. And I won't marry unless he's the right man. My mom says I'm too independent for most men. Well, actually, she said 'any man,' but I'm sure the right guy will love me, even if I'm a bit too ambitious."

Jake neared her ear and whispered, "There are some men who like that in a woman."

This time it was Ellen who stopped dancing. She took half a step back and asked, "Someone like you?" ending her question with a squeak of shock.

"Come on. Move your feet. People are staring at us," he said, winking. He pulled her closer. "Yes, people like me."

***

One month later

"One last chance to back out," her mother said. "I know how strong-willed you are. Jake's a nice kid…"

"Mom, he's a man. I love him, he loves me. He has a decent job and doesn't mind me working so we can buy a house. What's wrong? Don't you want me to be happy?"

"It's just this isn't how I thought you'd wind up."

"What, happy? Come on, Mom. Staying at home gardening, and canning tomatoes isn't for everyone. The world's changing. Mark my words, one of these days, women are going to be lawyers, even judges. Who knows? Maybe one day there'll be a woman in the Supreme Court."

"Pbbt! When pigs fly," Mom said. "Dreaming again, are you?"

Ellen shrugged. "You have to have a dream before you can chase it."

"Okay. So, my dream is for you to have at least two children: a boy and a girl. You can keep your job and I'll be the babysitter. I can't afford a nice gift, but that ought to be worth something. At least, if you do decide to have babies."

"Mom, you know as well as I do, babies come when they're ready. Until they figure out a miracle way to stop them."

"Well, you can always…"

"And don't say cross my legs. That joke was old when granny told it to you before we were born."

Chapter 3: Thirty-five Years Later

December 5, 1980

"Can't we bring her home, Dad?" Jon asked. "Hospitals are so...so...sterile."

"They're supposed to be, son," Jake said. "It's what's best for her, and right now, that's all I care about."

"How's Mom?" Genie asked, coming in with little Jacob on her hip.

Jake clenched his molars and huffed. "You know, for once I'd like to be able to give you two good news about your mother, but I can't. She's so far out of it now, she's either sleeping or talking to imaginary friends from her childhood. The doctor told me it's because she isn't getting enough oxygen to her brain."

"Why don't they just crank up the numbers?" Jon asked.

"She's at maximum now. She might have a day, maybe a week left. I just came back to shower and change clothes. You two can go see her if you'd like, but I doubt she'll know who you are. I want you to remember her as the strong, vibrant, and independent woman who made a difference in this town."

"Yeah, Ellen Johnson, the first female postmaster of McNeal. That was pretty cool," Genie said. "Who cares that she wasn't the first in the United States? She was a role model to me and lots of other girls in school."

"And that's how I want her to stick in your head. I won't think any less of either one of you if you stay here."

Ring, ring, ring.

"That's our line," Jon said. "Hello? Yes, he's right here."

Jake took the phone from his son, noticing he had his eyes down, intentionally avoiding him.

"Who was that?" Genie whispered to her brother.

"The doc at the hospital," he whispered back. "I don't think it's good news."

Jake dropped the phone and backed up to the big easy chair, dropping into it with a controlled fall, his eyes red. He sniffed back the tears. "She waited until I was away to die. Always looking out for me, trying to spare my feelings, weren't you Ellen?"

"Yes, she was," Genie said, rushing to his side to comfort him. "Don't worry, Dad. We're here for you. I'll stay as long as you need me."

Jake looked up at her and half-smiled at her remark. "Just like your mother, aren't you?"

"Yes, and no. I'll help, but she didn't stay long enough to finish her job of caring for you. I guess she passed the torch to Jon and me."

"No, you two are welcome to stay here with me, but only for a week or so. Helping me get the funeral arranged and going through some of her stuff would be very appreciated. You're both adults now and have lives of your own. Give me a little time to grieve, and I'm sure I'll be fine." He reached out and rubbed baby Jacob's sparse hair. "And you, daughter, have a son to take care of."

Jon cleared his throat to get his father's attention.

"And yes, pretty soon you'll have a family, too, I'm sure," Jake added, then pulled out his handkerchief and wiped his nose. "At least Ellen is no longer in pain and is with the Lord. I guess it's true: grieve for those left behind, not those who have departed."

"Focus on taking care of yourself, Dad. Life as a bachelor will be different, but you've done it before," Genie said.

"Um, not really. I pretty much went from high school to the Marines to being married to your mother. This is new territory for me," Jake said.

"Trust me, Dad," Jon said. "You got this. Before you know it – a year or two – you'll be dating again."

"Didn't do much of that, either," Jake said. "I had one girlfriend all through high school, then met your mom within a week of going home. Dating and being a bachelor are both as strange as setting up camp on Mars to me."

"Like Jon said, 'You got this.' Now, first things first. Go get cleaned up. I'll finish dinner. We can eat as an almost family after your shower."

"No, Genie. We're not an almost family – we're still a family. This is just the latest adjustment." Jake nodded to young Jacob. "The circle of life. One comes in, and one goes out. I'm sure glad she got a grandchild before she left."

Chapter 4: The Return of Mary

June 14, 1976

"I'm so glad you came for a visit, Mary," Linda said, taking a baking sheet of cookies out of the oven. "We have so much to catch up on. First, though, how is your mother?"

"She's tough as nails. She doesn't need me, but I think she asked me to come to stay with her because I've been in a funk. Losing two husbands in six years is taxing."

"You were married twice?" Linda asked, her eyes wide.

"Um, yes. Walter – the realtor from Douglas I married when I thought Jake was dead or didn't care about me anymore – didn't die, at least while I was married to him. We divorced after two years. He was a philandering so and so. He kept denying it, saying my friends were wrong, that the ladies he was practically seducing in restaurants were clients. I guess he was literally kissing up to them to close a deal. The last time, though, I caught him. When he tried to deny their relationship – with her sitting right next to him, his lips on her neck – she blew up. I guess he'd been telling her I was a fat drunken slob who lay around all day watching game shows and eating booze-filled bonbons, that he was going to divorce me as soon the kids were out of elementary school."

"I didn't know you had children."

"*We* didn't. It was all lies. Oh, and she recognized me from working at the newspaper. She apologized to me, slapped him hard on the face, and told him any man who'd dump a woman like me was too stupid for her. She and I wound up being good friends. When she moved to Idaho, we sort of lost track. She married a guy with four kids and then had four more with him. She was pretty busy after that. And happy."

"And your other husband?"

"Bill was a decent guy, but a workaholic. We had a son together. Tom's a firefighter in California. His dad was the top salesman for an insurance company, driving all over the country, looking for new clients, and working long hours. They kept trying to get him to slow down – told him according to their actuary, he would die at an early age if he didn't get his blood pressure and stress levels down. Well, they were right. He left me with a few bucks, but a hollowness in my gut. He wasn't around as much as I would have liked, but I always knew he'd be home in a few days. And then he was gone forever."

"When did he die?"

"A year ago, almost five years to the day after Walter died. My mother tells me I should start dating again. I don't know, though. I'm too old to start over."

Linda laughed. "Well, maybe to start having babies, but not to get a grandpa for those grandbabies Tom is going to give you."

"He's a confirmed bachelor."

"Or so he says," Linda said. "Speaking of bachelors, would you help me finish decorating these cookies today? It's Flag Day and I baked a few dozen sugar cookies. I could use a hand with the red, white, and blue icing."

"Might as well. We can chat and frost cookies at the same time."

***

Two hours later

"I can't believe how many you made," Mary said. "What are you going to do with all of them?"

"Deliver them to all the veterans in the area. Can you help me with that, too?" Linda asked.

"This many?"

"I'll take about half of them to the VFW, but the rest are going to be hand-delivered with a personal thank you note. I already made the cards and have my list of names and addresses, written down in location order so it should only take about an hour, maybe less."

Mary looked down at her powdered sugar and frosting-speckled clothes. "But I'm a mess. And I still have curlers in my hair."

"So?"

Mary rolled her eyes. "As long as you're the one getting out and handing them to the vets, I'm good with that. I'll drive and you deliver. Deal?"

"How about deal unless I run into a situation," Linda said, biting back her Cupid grin.

"Fair enough."

An hour and a half later, Mary asked, "How many more? I'm bushed."

"Just one," Linda said. "Keep going and I'll tell you where to turn."

"You'd better not be up to what I think you're up to. He's married," Mary said.

"Jake's wife died before Christmas of last year. Six months is long enough to grieve. I see him at church every Sunday. I can see the difference. He's ready to get on with his life, and by you being here, I'd say you were, too."

"Linda, you had this in mind all day, didn't you?"

"No, not really. You popped in while I was baking, remember? Let's just say it was kismet that you came by when you did. I just did a little fine-tuning with the order of deliveries, saving Jake for last."

Mary slowed down as they approached Johnson Road, the access to the property Jake's grandfather had homesteaded nearly a hundred years before. "I don't think I can do this. I'll wait in the car."

"Okay," Linda said.

"What? You're not going to argue with me?" Mary asked.

"Nope. If you don't want a chance at happiness, that's your decision."

"But I do. I just don't want to see him for the first time in… Oh, my Lord. We're here. It's been almost forty years since I've been here, and it looks just the same. Well, the house looks smaller because the trees are bigger. But other than that…"

Mary put the car in park and stared. It was twilight but still enough light to see the old turquoise-painted adobe house, the same white-washed wooden fence with metal gate, the hand-carved sign 'Johnson' tied to it with wire. The sign was yellow with black lettering now instead of stained wood as it had been when she'd last seen it. She wasn't positive, but it looked like the same one Jake had carved as a Christmas gift for his mother the year before he left.

Linda opened the car door. "Coming?" she asked.

"You go ahead. I'm not sure," Mary said, biting her thumbnail. She realized what she was doing and took it out. "Go ahead. I'll catch up. Maybe."

"Cluck, cluck, cluck. Chicken," Linda said, then shut the door, walking as slowly as she could to the house.

"Oh, shoot," Mary hissed, then got out, catching up to Linda as she knocked on the door.

Jon answered the door and asked them to come in. He recognized Linda from church, but the other woman was a stranger. "Here, let me turn off the TV. Nothing but junk on, anyhow. Genie, why don't you tell Dad that Linda and her friend are here. He's in the shop, finishing up that rocking horse for Jacob."

"Here, Genie," Linda said, handing Mary the plate of cookies then reaching for the toddler. "My, my, you're getting big, Jacob."

"Kids have a habit of doing that," Jon said. "Whatcha got there?" he asked, glancing at the cookies, then back up at her kerchief-covered head.

Mary held the plate so he could see it, ignoring his stare. "Cookies. Sort of a thank you for your service treat for your father. They're for Flag Day."

"Oops," Linda said. "I forgot to introduce you. Mary, this is Jon, Jake's son. This fine young boy is Jacob, and his mother Genie – Jake and Ellen's oldest – just went to get her dad. You remember Jake, don't you?"

Mary blushed scarlet, her color shades darker than the pinkness

26

of her curlers. "Yes, I do," she answered, her teeth clenched as she glared at her friend.

"Hi, Linda," Jake said, coming in from the back door, the handmade rocking horse project in his hand. He looked to her left and dropped the wooden toy. "Mary?"

"Well, I guess your eyes are still good," Mary answered with a shrug, then self-consciously started buttoning her loose cotton overshirt, covering her tank top. "But not too good, I hope."

"What…why…I mean, last I heard you moved to Nevada," Jake said, walking towards her in a daze.

"Nevada? That was thirty-five years ago. Oh… Yes. Sorry about that. I really did think you died, and when the letters stopped, I… I did keep writing, though, just in case."

Jake walked toward her across the long room as she babbled in embarrassment. He let her continue, grinning the whole time.

"Why are you smiling?"

"You're just as beautiful as ever."

"What? Me?" Her hands flew up to her curlers. "I take it back about your eyes."

"Too late." He took the plate of cookies from her. "Christmas cookies?"

"Not only are your eyes bad, I think you must be blind!" Mary said, sniffling back the tears of joy at seeing him again.

"Blinded by beauty," he said softly, raising the plate to toast her with it, then setting it back lower so he could see the decorations on the cookies without his glasses. "Red, white, and blue?"

"It's Flag Day," Mary said.

"Yeah, thanks for your service, Dad," Jon said with a tinge of sarcasm.

Jake spun around and glared. "What did you say?" he asked.

"Um, thanks for putting your life on the line and defending our country," Jon said, his chagrin evident in his remorseful voice.

"Thousands of men and women lost their lives in that war," Jake said, his voice booming. "Thousands more have died in wars before and since. All to make sure you can make snippy remarks about them."

"I'm sorry, Dad. Really, I am. I know better. It's just, what's she doing here? And why are you all googly-eyed all of a sudden?"

"Jon, you embarrass me. I know you know Linda from church. She brought a friend over, and this is how you treat her? Your mother and I brought you up better than that."

"Dad," Genie interrupted. "You're right, but he has a valid point. Why are you acting so weird?"

"Your father and I dated in high school," Mary said.

"More than dated," Jake said. "I asked her to marry me on December sixth, 1941. Two days later – the day after Pearl Harbor – I joined the Marines. We kind of lost track when I was over there."

"But what about Mom?" Jon asked. "I thought she was your one and only."

"I knew your mother as a child. When I got back from the war, she and I met at a mixer dance – one the locals put on so the women could meet the guys who'd been overseas. A month later, we were married. But she was not the first woman I asked to marry me."

Jake set the cookies on the sideboard. "Genie, would you start

28

some coffee and bring out some plates. I'd like to catch up for a few minutes."

"Hmph," Jon snorted.

"I think you need to leave, Jon," Jake said. "Come back when you rediscover your manners. I know you used to have them. It's a shame you lost them."

Mary shrank back close to the bookcase, trying to be unobtrusive as the angry young man grabbed his ball cap and left through the front door, walking within inches of her, his scowl seeming to send out hate rays.

"Don't worry about him," Jake said, picking up and fluffing the throw pillow on the overstuffed chair in the corner. "Sit down and let's chat while the coffee's brewing. Oh, Linda," he said as an afterthought, "make yourself comfortable."

"I think I'll help Genie in the kitchen while you two catch up."

"Suit yourself," Jake said, then brought the ottoman next to Mary.

"What was that all about or do I want to know?" Mary asked.

"I guess he thinks I should morn his mother until it's time for my funeral. Kids. He's young and thinks he knows it all. He'll be leaving by the weekend. He and his girlfriend had a spat. He's letting her cool down. Or so he says. I think it's the other way around. Either way, he's emotional."

"Oh," Mary said, stunned and uncomfortable. "I guess that happens."

Jake patted Mary's knee in assurance. "Don't worry about him," he said, then left his hand where it was. "Oh, and I have to tell you. I found out the mystery of the missing letters."

"What mystery?"

"As you know, you and I were writing letters. There was another Jake Johnson in the battalion, but I never interacted with him. I guess he was intercepting my mail – or at least some of it. I learned later that he was a clerk and handled the correspondence. He let the letters from my congressman and mother come through, but the ones that smelled good and had sealed-with-a-kiss written on the back, he took for himself. I guess he justified it with we both had the same name."

"But I never got any of yours," Mary said.

"He also took care of outgoing mail. He had to make sure he didn't get caught, so he stopped my outbound letters. He could have been sent to jail for what he did, but by then I was too out of it with malaria to press charges. Not that it would do any good. You'd already sent the Dear John letter. That was what made him stop the thefts and interceptions. He realized he'd messed up a romance by trying to live someone else's life vicariously. He returned the letters to me when I was in the hospital. He sent word that he wanted to buy me a beer but couldn't, so he sent me a bottle of Coke. I still have it, too."

"Oh, my God." Mary grabbed Jake's hand and brought it to her mouth and kissed it. "I'm so sorry. I should have waited…"

"It is what it is. It's no one's fault but the other Jake Johnson's. You had to move on. When I got back, I did, too. I had nearly thirty-five wonderful years with Ellen. We had two mostly great children," he rolled his eyes, looking to the door Jon had just left through, "and Ellen got a chance to see her first grandchild before she died."

"Ahem," Genie cleared her throat loudly. "Catching up, eh, Dad?"

"Not at all," he said. "just explaining a mystery."

"Looks more like a romance," Genie said, cups, and saucers in hand, her narrow-eyed glare almost identical to her brother's.

"Lighten up, Genie," Linda said, coming in with the coffee carafe and a bundle of napkins. "They're both adults and single. And last I heard, this was still his house. He can do whatever he likes in it. Within reason," she added with a wink.

"But Mom died less than a year ago," Genie protested.

"Yes," Linda said, taking one of the cups. "And I'm sure she's not coming back. She always wanted to make him happy. Giving him another chance at love is what she'd want."

"Ahem," Jake interjected. "Looks like you're ready to be a witness at our wedding, and Mary's been here less than fifteen minutes."

"Yeah, well," Linda said, not even trying to contain her self-righteous smirk, "sometimes that's all it takes."

"Yes, Linda, I'd love a cup of coffee," Mary said, hoping to break the tension. "Cream or milk if you have it. No sugar, though."

Jake leaned in and whispered, "Still sweet enough?" then sat back and blushed. "Did I just say that?"

"Yeah, Dad. We all heard it," Genie said with a harsh edge to her voice. "I think I'll take Jacob outside for a walk. Maybe it'll wear him out enough to get to sleep."

"See if you can find a better attitude while you're out there," Jake said. "It seems like whatever Jon had is catching."

"Ach, don't worry about them," Linda said, pouring a splash of cream into Mary's cup of coffee. "They'll either get over it or they'll spend less time here. It's time they grew up, too."

Jake wriggled his shoulders like he was trying to get out of a tight spot. "You're right. They have been spending a lot of time here. They need to get on with their own lives."

Jake put one hand on Mary's knee again, grinning at the sensation, glad that she wasn't upset with him, then looked into her eyes. "I don't know where this is going, but I'm so glad you dropped in." Mary's hand automatically went up to touch her rollers again. "And I wouldn't care if you were bald or still a brunette, you're still beautiful."

"Silver highlights look good on you," Linda said. "And you kept your figure. I guess you don't bake too many cookies then, do you?"

"Only for special occasions," Mary said.

"Got any plans for the Fourth of July?" Jake asked. "If I remember right, you had a heck of a good recipe for snickerdoodles."

"And jam thumbprints. Maybe next time we can spend a little time in the kitchen."

"Catch up on old recipes?"

"Hey, you two," Linda said. "I'm sitting right here."

Jake and Mary both looked at her and grinned. "Probably a good thing, too," Jake said.

"Or not," Mary added, patting Jake's hand that still rested on her knee. She sighed and repeated, "Or not."

Chapter 5: Goodbye Until Tomorrow

"Are you sure you have to leave so soon?" Jake asked.

"Don't worry, she'll be back, I'm sure," Linda said.

Mary rolled her eyes at her friend. "I think Genie wants to put Jacob down for the night. I'm just down the road at Mom's. I'm glad she bought back the old place. You can contact me there."

Jake looked at his watch. "Yeah, Genie wasn't too subtle, was she? I have to work tomorrow, but I get off at three-thirty. Give me a little bit of time to clean up and we can go for a ride. You know, check out all the old places, see what's changed and what's the same?"

"I can see one thing hasn't changed," Linda quipped. "Oh, and no, I can't come with you tomorrow. I...um...have a prior engagement. The laundry and I have a standing date at four, but you two go along and have a good time without me. I already know what's changed and what's stayed the same since I haven't left since I was born."

"One thing that hasn't changed is your sense of humor, Linda," Mary said. "I don't know how I lived so long without having you around to pepper the air with sassiness."

"Happy to be your jalapeño, Mary. Come on, you two. I'll wait in the car while you say your good nights. Don't take too long, though."

Linda patted Jake on the shoulder, then let herself out the front door, grinning like a drunken Cupid at her success.

"Do you feel like you were set up, Jake?" Mary asked.

"What? You mean by Linda? Nah. She and I are pals. She's bugged me about coming to some of the senior mixers with her over in Sierra Vista, but as her friend, not her date."

"Do you mean she's invited you out?"

"Not that way. Believe me. I may be getting old, but I know when a woman is interested. I know she'd like to find a tick for her tock, but it's not me." Jake shuddered. "Ew. Just the thought of the two of us... She's like my sister. Nah, her beau will come, but it certainly isn't me."

"So," Mary said, drawing out her question, "does that mean the thought of me gives you the chills?"

"Yes, but not the same way. You'd better go before my daughter brings out the shotgun." Jake nodded to the reflection in the glass of the door. Genie was standing in the kitchen doorway, arms crossed, glaring.

Eyes wide, Mary immediately canceled her idea for a chaste goodnight kiss and instead held out her hand to shake his. "I'll see you tomorrow around four-thirty then," she said.

"Maybe sooner," Jake whispered, holding her hand. "And I'll make sure I don't have a chaperone."

***

All day long, Jake kept looking at his watch, willing the hands to go faster. Stomach in knots, he skipped lunch and took his half-hour break at the end of the day. He was off the airfield and into his truck by five after three, home and in and out of the shower by three-thirty.

Five minutes later, a nervous sweat competing with summer perspiration, he rang Mrs. Decker's doorbell. He quickly wiped the back of his hand across his forehead, drying it on the side of his jeans.

"Well, that was quick," Mary said, her hair coifed and makeup perfect. "Come in and say hi to Mom before we leave." She leaned in and whispered, "She's been talking about you all day."

"There's my boy," Mrs. Decker said, waving her cane at him. "I see you around town every once in a while, but ever since I stopped going to church, I don't get a chance to sit and chit chat."

"Mom," Mary said, "he came to pick me up so we could go for a drive, not so you two could talk about old times. Besides, it's your own fault for losing faith and not going to church."

"Don't you know, Mrs. Decker, that it's when you *don't* want to go to church that you need it the most?" Jake asked.

She blinked in shock. "Well... Maybe so. But when the Lord took her father, I was mad at him. Still am."

Jake chuckled. "At least you still call him Lord and acknowledge he's the One in charge. There's hope for you. We'll all say a prayer for you next Sunday. I'll start tonight, just to make sure you're covered."

Mrs. Decker reached out her cane and tapped his leg playfully. "You do that. And ask for a new hip, too."

"He can do that. You know they replace them now, don't you?" Jake asked.

"Yeah, but I have to have my blood pressure down first."

35

"And why is it high? No, wait. I'll bet it's because you stress too much, right?"

"Well, maybe…"

"Don't you know if you turn it over to God, you won't have to worry? He's got mighty broad shoulders, I hear."

"Go ahead and take him on that ride, will you, Mary? I just got a year's worth of preaching in two minutes. I don't think I can handle any more."

"Come on, Jake, let's go." Mary picked up her purse, looked inside to make sure she had everything she needed, then stepped over to her mother. "Behave yourself, Mom. And he's right: stop stressing. If I can't take care of it, I'll ask Jake or Linda for help. And if they can't, well, we have call forwarding," she said, looking up to heaven.

Mrs. Decker pursed her lips and shook her head in a light-hearted scold. "Git, git! Don't have too much fun… No, on second thought, have all the fun you want. You have to make up for thirty-five years apart."

"Mo-om!" Mary said softly, a blush rising.

"Don't worry, Mrs. Decker. You know me – I'll be respectful."

"Well, not too respectful, I hope," she replied. "The girl is due to have a little fun."

Mary grunted and rushed out the door, knowing Jake would follow. When he showed up to join her in the truck a half-minute later, she said, "I swear she gets her kicks out of embarrassing me."

"Yes, I think she does. What else does she have for entertainment?"

"Where's a dirty old man when you need one?" Mary asked.

"I hope that was a rhetorical question because if not, we can always put out the word at the VFW."

"Don't you dare, Jake," Mary said, then laughed. "You're right, though. She needs to get out more."

"What about you?" Jake asked. "Are you going to stick around for a while? I mean, to put it bluntly, I'm interested. But we're both burning wax off the old candle of life. I'd hate to get all wound up and find out you're leaving on Monday for your job in Africa or Australia or somewhere else far from Cochise County."

"Wow," she said. She pointed to the ignition. "If we're in such a hurry, we'd better get going on our tour of the old sites while we can still see."

"I'm sorry if that came out wrong," Jake said, starting the truck. "Tell me what I said isn't the truth, though."

"Well, I'm not going overseas, or even anywhere else. I took an early retirement from the newspaper. One of those hard to refuse offers when the small press I was working for was bought out by one of the big boys. I didn't know where to go, thought Mom might need me, so popped down here until I could figure out what I wanted to write in the next chapter of my life."

She looked back at him for his reaction and saw his smile growing, the truck still in gear. "Are we going somewhere or not?"

"I sure hope so," he said, putting it in first. "I sure hope so."

***

The two spent an hour driving down the small country roads, Jake pointing out the old greenhouse in disrepair, the cemetery sign hanging sideways from the last windstorm, the new modular homes sprouting up on former pasture lands.

"I see the old Douglas landmark is still there," Mary said.

"Oh, the smelter?" Jake asked. "Yeah, environmentalists are going after them. I don't mind it as long as the wind's blowing the smoke into Mexico."

"Pbbt. That's rude. So, I told you about my plans. What are yours?"

"I could retire pretty much any time I want. It would be at seventy percent rate, but I've got enough put away that I could survive and even have a little fun. No reason to, though. I'd just be bored at home all day. I can only cut and carve so much wood. I'm about overrun with bookcases as it is."

"I saw that little rocking horse last night. Was that one you made?"

"Just something I was playing around with. Jacob started walking last month. I figured if I built one sized to him, he could get on and off it without getting hurt. I haven't figured out how to make the mane yet, though."

"How about a rag mop? I mean, buy a new mophead, dye it, and then glue or staple it in place."

"Yeah, and it'd give him something to grab onto when he was riding it. Great idea. Wanna go into a partnership?"

"Sure, why not?" Mary said. "No. Wait. Aren't I supposed to play a little hard to get before you ask me?"

"What? Oh, you little minx. No, I did not just ask you to marry me," Jake said, pretending to be angry, frowning, his voice low.

"So, you don't want to marry me?" Mary asked.

"Well, yes, I do. I mean… Mary, dag nab it, you did it again, didn't you? You got me to ask you for your hand in marriage."

"I didn't hear anything about hands, but I did hear you ask me to be your partner without any prompting at all."

"Partnership," Jake corrected.

"So, what's the difference?"

"Partners are two people who work together," Jake said. "A partnership is an accepted or legal arrangement where two people work together toward a common goal. Or something like that."

"So, I suggested partner – which wouldn't have any long-term commitment – but you asked me to go into a partnership with you. Would it be a legal arrangement or just casual?"

Jake pulled into a long drive that led to one of the dozens of ranches on the roller coaster main road. He put the truck in neutral and turned to her. "I hope this means you want to be seriously involved because I really do miss you. I mean, this banter back and forth. It's filling holes I didn't even know I had."

"As in you complete me?" Mary asked.

"Yes. That's a great way to put it."

Mary reached out and held his hand. "I know what you're talking about because I feel it, too. It's as if all the years shrunk down into days – like we've only been apart for a month, not decades."

Jake put one finger up in the air to stop her as she neared him for a kiss. "I didn't do it in the right order last time, so let me try again. First, Mary Decker Whatever-your-other-last-name-is-now, I love you. Will you marry me?"

"I love you, too, Jake The-real-one-not-the-letter-stealing-one Johnson." She leaned in and kissed him, tingles going up her arms as their lips touched, then pulled back.

"What? Did I move too fast?" Jake asked.

"Uh-uh. I forgot to say yes. So, yes, Jake, I'll marry you," she said, then whispered, "Now, where were we?"

"Right about here…"

Chapter 6: The Barbecue

"You what?" Genie screeched, startling young Jacob and making him cry. She put her hand on his head and pulled him close to her shoulder. "It's okay, sweetheart. Mommy just got a little scared." She glimpsed at Mary, then glared at her father as she picked up the diaper bag on her way out the door. "We have to leave. See you later. Maybe."

"Well, that went over like the proverbial turd in the punch bowl," Jake said. "I didn't expect immediate approval, but I didn't expect that, either."

"You'd think she'd understand, being a wife and all," Mary said.

"Wife? Her boyfriend knocked her up and left the state. Turns out he had a wife and five kids. She's better off without him and she knows it. Still, it's been tough. That's why she spends so much time over here," Jake said.

"Does she have a job? Friends?"

"No and yes. There aren't any jobs around here. Besides, even if she could find one, what would she do for daycare? Nah, she's stuck on welfare. Friends? They're either single and clueless about kids and responsibilities or have families of their own and are too busy for her. I'm it."

"So, she's jealous of my time with you. Or the time we'll have together."

Honk! Honk!

"Probably. That's Jon. Maybe he'll take it a little better. By the way, what did Tom say when you told him?"

"He said, 'Third time's a charm, Mom,' then 'Gotta go. Just got a call.' He's busy enough that as long as I'm safe and happy, he doesn't care what I do."

"How'd you get so lucky?" Jake asked, watching Jon get out of his Jeep.

"He's a workaholic like his dad. At least he has to stay close to home and his workdays are spaced far apart. Firefighters are lucky that way."

Jake put his hand on Mary's shoulder as Jon walked in the front door. "Good afternoon, Jon. I'm glad you could join us. I figured it was a fine day for a barbecue. I got some nice rib eye steaks, and Mary's made a ton of potato salad and a couple of apple pies, too."

"You know me, Dad. I'll never turn down free food, even if I have to do the dishes."

"Oh, don't worry about dishes. I'll take care of them," Mary said. "Would you like something to drink?"

"Anything cold and alcoholic will do," Jon said.

"Got you covered," Mary said. She turned away and looked at Jake, grimacing.

"Mary also set up a tray of veggies for us," Jake said, nodding to the table laid out with radish roses, carrot curls, and celery sticks stuffed with cream cheese.

"What? No chips and onion dip? What's a party without them?"

"We're going for healthy, son. When you get to be our age,

42

eating right just makes sense."

"Well, I'm not old. At least, not that old." Jon accepted the beer from Mary. "Just don't tell me you invited me over so you could tell me you're getting married."

Jon popped the top and was taking a long swig of beer, waiting for their answer. When neither of them spoke, he brought the can down, having swallowed half in the first gulp. "You didn't ask her, did you?"

"Yes, I did. As a matter of fact, we're getting married next weekend. It will just be a small..."

Jon slammed the can down on the table, sloshing its contents over his hand and the tablecloth. "Dammit, Dad. You've only been dating, what? A week? Three or four days?"

"I married your mother a month after I got back from the war. I've known Mary a lot longer than that, plus we dated for years in high school. It's not as if..."

Jon turned to leave, remembered his beer, grabbed it, and headed towards the door. "I think you're making the biggest mistake of your life," he said, then slammed the door behind him, cracking the glass in one of the windowpanes.

"Well, that didn't go well," Mary said.

Jake shrugged. "His loss."

"Really? That's it?" Mary stared at him, took a deep breath, then went into the kitchen to get a dishcloth. "I mean, I expected a little resistance," she said as she wiped up the spilled beer, "but he's got more rage than I ever could have imagined."

"As I said, his loss." Jake sat down and pulled out the chair next

43

to him, patting it for her to join him. "He's not as mad at me as he is at himself. He had a nice girl and blew it. He chose beer over her one too many times. Now, love is coming so quick and easy for me, he's jealous. It's his choice to be out of our lives. He'll come around, or he won't."

"What about Genie?"

"Sort of the same thing. She missed out on getting her happy ever after, too. Hers is different because it wasn't her fault. She still doesn't have anyone, though. Well, except for a thirteen-month-old who poops his pants and won't sleep all night."

"So, what are we going to do?" Mary asked.

"Eat a lot of potato salad and veggies," Jake said dryly.

"No, really."

"Yes, really. What we're going to do is get on with our lives. They're both adults. They'll get their chance. In the meantime, I'm not giving up on mine just to make them happy...or less angry. Shoot! I'm into making me happy. And you, too, of course."

"Well, then, I'd say it's a barbecue for two unless you want to call a few friends over," Mary said. "We certainly have enough food."

"Maybe Linda wants to come. Maybe she can scare up a plus one."

"Doesn't cost anything to check since it's a local call. I'm on it."

***

"Thanks for the invitation," Linda said. "And would you stop apologizing for being last minute? I was wondering what we were going to do today. Plus, I've wanted to introduce you to Scooter. He

44

and I have been acquainted for a while. We both volunteer at the museum on post but our hours never really coincided. I knew him by name, not sight, but he'd seen me around and was interested. Well, I guess he asked for a shift change so he could meet me, and next thing you know, we're on a date."

"And you didn't tell me?" Mary whispered.

"I didn't want to jinx it. Shush. Here he comes."

"I don't like coming to a party empty-handed," the mustached man said, an enormous watermelon held close to his chest.

Mary looked down then back up as she realized she was staring.

"Yup, they're mine. Bought and paid for and custom-sized," he said, then chuckled, trying to ease her discomfort. "Bright and shiny, save me a fortune on pedicures, but darn near worthless when swimming."

"Oh, I'm sorry. Where are my manners?" Linda said. "Mary, this is Scooter Gibbons. Scooter, this is Mary, my best friend since high school. She just got engaged. Come in and meet the lucky guy."

"Let me take that," Mary said. "I've been dying to try out a new way to cut these up. If I do it right, it'll look like a basket of melon balls when I'm done."

"Be careful," Scooter said. "It's heavier than it looks."

He gently rolled it into her arms, her elbows ready to cradle it. "Yes, and I'm stronger than I look, too," she answered, accepting it with ease. "Oh, and Jake's out back cutting up some mesquite branches. He says the smoke gives the meat a better flavor than charcoal."

"I can't argue there," Scooter says. "Not that I'm a snob or would

45

turn down a good steak from anywhere, but I have to tell you, I'm glad he's not using a gas grill."

"Oh, good grief," Linda said. "You are too a snob. I can't tell the difference."

"Well, that means your good taste only runs in men, then," Scooter said and gave her a quick kiss.

"Oh, you…" she said, swatting at him playfully, her face suddenly reddening.

"Linda, you're blushing," Mary said. "On second thought, I'll save this project for when we're done with dinner. We can have it for our second dessert after apple pie. I want to stick around and get to know the man who can embarrass you."

"Embarrass her? Nah," Scooter said. "I'm just setting loose her inner glow. It's been stifled for so long, it comes out in bursts."

"More like flashes," Linda said and giggled.

"You said it, I didn't," Mary quipped, leading the way to the backyard and picnic table. She looked up and saw Jake bringing in the wood he had cut up using the table saw in the shop.

"When you get your arms unloaded there, Jake," Linda said, "I have someone I'd like to introduce you to."

"What? You found someone willing to hang around you for more than a minute," Jake teased, then looked up. His eyes widened and arms slackened, dropping the load of fresh-cut mesquite into a tangled pile at his feet.

"Scooter?" Jake gasped.

"Jake? I mean, I thought you were in prison," Scooter said, walking up to greet him, both arms out.

46

Jake enveloped him in a bear hug, swinging him side to side, then both men patted each other on the shoulder with the 'that's enough' gesture.

"Prison? Why would I be in prison?" Jake asked.

"I looked you up a few years ago after my," Scooter looked down at his missing legs. "Well, I had some time on my hands, so I called around. I gave the VA your name and our division and battalion. They told me you'd been convicted of mail fraud and sentenced to forty years in prison."

"Well, I'll be..." Jake said, then started laughing.

"So, it wasn't you, was it?" Scooter asked.

"No, I'll tell you about it in a minute. In the meantime, I'd like you to meet Mary. I'm sure you remember her. Or at least the name."

"Your Mary? *The* Mary?" Scooter asked.

"The one, the only."

"But Linda said Mary just got engaged."

"I was recently widowed. So was she. She came back to visit family and one thing led to another... And here you thought it wouldn't work out. It just took thirty-five years to come back to where it was supposed to be."

Jake looked around then realized that the picnic table might be awkward for Scooter to access. "Let me get you a real chair. These things are knee busters."

"No worries there," Scooter said. "Don't have knees, but a hardback chair would be easier to get in and out of. Camp chairs are the worst."

Jake went into the house and brought out a kitchen chair. "Does anyone care for a cool one?"

"I got this," Linda said. "I know what you like, Scooter." She reached into the cooler and brought out a lemon-lime soda. "Your non-caffeine mixer without the booze."

Jake took the soda Mary handed him and squinted at Scooter, waiting for the story that he was sure his old Army buddy wanted to share.

"I was the designated driver that night. Not a taste of liquor passed my lips. I was driving my three buddies back to our apartment complex when *bam!* A drunk driver ran a stop sign. Killed two of my friends, the other was messed up pretty bad but recovered, and I lost both legs. Ironically, the drunk driver only got a few scratches and a broken arm. He was let off with six months in jail for manslaughter. Now, what's fair about that?"

"You and I know that life's not fair," Jake said. "Do you know why you thought I was in prison?" Scooter shrugged and Linda brought over a five-gallon bucket and turned it upside down to sit next to him.

"There was another guy named Jake Johnson in our battalion. He was a clerk. He was stealing all my letters from Mary for himself. I guess he was pretending she was his sweetheart or something. To cover his tracks, he intercepted my outbound mail. She kept writing, I did, too, but neither one of us got the letters. What happened there? She thought I didn't care or had been killed. Was that fair?"

Mary cleared her throat and Jake nodded to her. "I knew only death or a severe injury would keep him from writing to me. I never figured on mail fraud."

"And yet we still found each other. True, we missed thirty-five years, but we're both young and healthy enough that, Lord willing, we have thirty-five more years ahead of us."

Scooter ran one finger up and down the sweaty can, flipping the dewy drops into the trees. "So, do you know why I was here in Cochise County?" Scooter asked.

"I have to say I'm mighty curious," Jake said.

"You painted such a beautiful picture of this part of the country. Slower pace, wide-open spaces," he patted Linda on the leg, "fabulous women... I was stuck with two-thirds of a body and a broken spirit. I was ready to start over again. I figured if it was that special to you, maybe it would be for me, too. I couldn't find a place to buy out here and didn't want to sit around and do nothing all day. The Army being in my blood, I wound up at Fort Huachuca. I rented an apartment, got involved with the VFW, and got talked into volunteering at the museum. I noticed this sassy little gal here leaving work one day, asked around, got told I was a creeper..."

"Oh, you did not," Linda said, smacking him on the upper arm. "My boss said if you wanted to know my name, you'd have to go up and ask me. So, you did."

"And darned glad of it, too," Scooter said. He leaned in and kissed her. "I think I'll stick around this area. I might even move closer to this neck of the desert if this lady wants me to hang around on a more permanent basis."

Linda giggled and asked, "Are you asking me to marry you, Scooter Gibbons?"

"Yes, I am. If you don't mind, I'd like to skip the getting down on one knee part, though. I don't believe I'd be able to get back up."

"I was joking," Linda said, eyes wide in shock.

"I wasn't. I was waiting to have witnesses, though. I didn't want you to balk on me and insist I was teasing."

Linda looked from Scooter to Mary to Jake, then back to Scooter. "Um, yes, I'll marry you. But I don't think I'll fit into my mother's old wedding gown anymore."

"Get married in a housecoat, jeans and a sweatshirt, or in the buff. I don't care. I do want to claim you before any of the other guys at the VFW find out you're single. We all thought you were married."

"But I'm not single," Linda said, a sparkle of mischief in her eye.

"Wha…what?" Scooter gasped.

"I'm spoken for," she said and kissed him. She pulled back from the long, slow kiss and added, "By you."

"Best women in the world," Scooter said, raising his fist in victory.

***

Two hours later, dinner was finished. The four-pack of friends realigned around the cut down fifty-gallon drum Jake had set up as a fire pit. "This should keep the mosquitoes down."

"Mesquite smells good even when it's not grilling beefsteak," Scooter said. "As you were saying, I guess it was meant to be. It took a break-me-down tragedy to kick myself out of my rut in the city. Don't tell anyone, but I was a lawyer."

Jake painted the letter T over his chest and said, "Cross my heart, hope to die."

"Too bad I couldn't be in charge of that drunk driver's trial. He was sentenced and had his time served before they could get a pair of legs that would work for me. Of course, his insurance company did pay for it all. They're still paying me, as a matter of fact. So, Linda, motorhome, trailer, or fifth-wheel to go touring the state?"

"Wait…what?" Linda gasped. When he started to repeat it, she held up her hand.

"Now what do we have here?" Jon asked, walking into the backyard with a drunken swagger.

"Ho-boy," Mary said under her breath. She looked at Jake and saw he was livid.

"Did you drive here?" Jake asked Jon.

"No… I flew. Of course, I drove here. Do you think I'd walk from the bar in Bisbee here? I wouldn't even be to the outshirts of town… I mean, the outshirps… I wouldna even be to the edge of town if I was on foot."

"Get in the house," Jake said, reaching out to usher Jon in by the elbow.

Jon waved his arms in the air in protest, slipping away from his father's near grasp. "I just wanted to say congratulations to the bribe and groom. I mean, the bride and gloom. I mean, to the happy couple. Mom's probably rolling over in her grave right now, and you're all shitting around, I mean sitting around, havin' a party."

"You're drunk, Jon. Get inside before you say something you'll regret."

"What? Don't I get to kish the bride?" Jon asked, looking at Mary, his lips pursed in an exaggerated pucker.

Mary turned away and ran into the house, realized it wasn't her home, and she didn't have a car to get back to her Mom's. She locked herself in the bathroom, then sat on the edge of the tub and sobbed, wondering what she could do.

"I am *not* going to apologize," Jon hollered, slamming chairs aside as he made his way through the old territorial house to the front door.

"Yes, you are. That was totally uncalled for," Jake bellowed.

"No, someone had to say something. Genie feels the same way except she's gutless."

"Maybe she feels the same way, but she has some tact. And she's not a drunk."

"I am not a drunk," Jon said. "I only drink beer. And I can stop anytime. I just don't want to." Jon opened the refrigerator door and moved food around, dropping the jar of mayonnaise on the floor before he found the last beer buried in the back. "Ah, one for the road."

"You're not leaving until you sober up," Jake said, resisting the urge to grab him.

Jon stepped up to him, nose to nose. "Watch me," he said and turned away.

This time, Jake reached out, catching Jon by the elbow. Jon spun on his heel, staggering to keep his balance, and threw a flimsy haymaker. Jake ducked and grabbed Jon's hand, causing him to drop the beer. Jon bent over and picked it up before it spilled.

"See, I got good free-flexes, I mean reflexes."

Scooter walked in the backdoor and stood in the kitchen,

watching the father-son confrontation. "I'll drive him home," he offered in a calm voice.

Jon looked down at his prosthetic legs then back up. "Nah, I got this," he said.

Jake started to hold him back again but saw Jon's glare and paused.

"If you hit me, it'll be the last thing you ever do, father or not," Jon said and walked out, slamming the door again, breaking the glass next to the newly replaced windowpane.

Jake sighed as he left. "I guess I'll have to put in plexiglass next time."

"Don't worry," Scooter said. "I disconnected his battery before I came in. As drunk as he is, he won't figure it out."

"Thanks. Put on your iron shorts, though. He's not done." Jake looked around. "Where's Mary?"

"Hiding," Mary said, coming out of the bathroom. "I think I'd better go home."

"You are home. Or it will be your home soon. Don't let him get to you. He's drunk," Jake said.

"It's Ellen's home. I don't think this could ever be our home. I'm tearing your family apart. The kids don't want me…"

"Whoa, whoa, whoa," Jake said, bringing his arm around her. "They're adults, remember? Lord, I wish they were as accepting as your son, but they're not. We'll get through this. Together."

"Please take me home," Mary said, wiping her tears with a paper napkin.

Vroom! Vroom!

53

"Shit," Jake said. "He's taking my truck!"

Scooter and Mary looked at him. "He has a spare key in case I get locked out," Jake said. "Damn it!"

"Is it okay to come in?" Linda asked.

"Oh, shoot," Mary said. "I'm sorry. It started out as a great party, especially the engagement part." Mary looked at Jake, eyes filled with tears. "I think I need to take a break. At least a little one to get this sorted out. Like you were saying, if it was meant to be, it'll all come together."

"Mary," Scooter said, "I just met you, but I know how much you mean to Jake. Someone came between you before; don't let it happen again."

Mary shook her head. "No, this isn't the same. This someone is his son. And his daughter. I won't be a homewrecker." She looked at the cracked glass in the front door. "Literally."

Chapter 7: Driving Under the Influence

The next day

Knock, knock.

Jake answered the door. "Why, hello, Sheriff. What brings you out here so early in the morning?"

"Sorry to be the bearer of bad news, Jake, but Jon's in the hospital. He ran your truck off the highway into the ditch. He was still pretty drunk by the time we got there. Good thing someone had a CB radio and called it in. He's pretty messed up. Your truck is a total loss, I'm afraid."

"Is he alive? Of course, he is. Is he going to live? Because if he is, I might kill him."

Jake looked around the living room then up at the sheriff. "Can you give me a ride to the hospital?" He patted his back pocket, made sure he had his wallet, then put up a finger. "Gotta turn off the coffee pot."

"What are you going to do for wheels?" the sheriff asked.

"I'm taking possession of his Jeep. He has the keys with him. I hope. If not, I'll put in a new ignition switch. I hope to hell he's not allowed behind the wheel for at least three years. That idiot. I tried to stop him, and he threw a punch. Took all I had not to throw one back. In hindsight, I guess I should have. He wouldn't be in the hospital and

I'd still have my truck."

"He's going to jail this time, Jake. This is his third offense."

"What?"

"I ran his name and license number. He got a DUI in Sedona last year. Spent the night in jail and paid a big fine. Add that to the one he got here in high school and that's three strikes. The laws are changing. This one isn't going to be cheap."

"Did he hurt anyone else?" Jake asked, locking the door behind him as they headed to the cruiser.

"Just the ditch. This time."

***

"Well, look who's the big man now," Jake said.

Jon looked up from his hospital bed, his broken leg in traction, ten stitches above his eyebrow, and two black eyes.

"By the double shiners, I'd say you broke your nose, too," Jake added, pulling up a chair to sit next to his somber son.

"Sounds like you have a little experience there," Jon said, his voice gravelly.

"My injuries were from fighting for freedom, not driving drunk. You deserve all you got and more. Oh, and thanks for the Jeep. It's mine until you get me a truck, but the payments are still yours."

"Dad, what's going to happen to me?" Jon asked, tears dribbling from the corners of his eyes into his sideburns.

"Jail time, probably loss of your job, maybe a limp for the rest of your life, exorbitant car insurance if they even let you drive again. Hmm. You already lost your girlfriend and, oh yeah...

56

Congratulations! You lost me my gal, too."

Jake stood up, angry all over again at the way Jon had treated Mary. He looked down at his son, pathetic in his broken state – both physical and emotional – then sat down again.

"You're lucky you got out with just a few dings and a broken leg. My friend you almost met yesterday, the man with prosthetic legs? He and I survived Iwo Jima and four years of fighting all over the Pacific. I came out whole; he lost a pinkie finger. Do you know how he lost his legs? Wait, I'm not going to let you guess. It was a drunk driver. He lost two friends in that accident. I hope to heaven and hell you never, ever drink again."

Jon sniffed, his silent sobs stealing his words.

"Not much you can say to that, is there, big boy? Yeah, I'm ashamed of you. But you're still my son and I love you. But if you ever so much as have one beer, I may disown you. I don't care what you say: if you drink every day – whether it's whiskey, wine, or beer – you're an alcoholic."

"But…but…"

"If you can't stop at one drink, you're an alcoholic. At least, in my book. And never, ever have one 'for the road.'"

"Knock, knock," Genie said, standing in the doorway. "Can we come in?"

"Hey, there. How's my favorite grandson," Jake said, taking Jacob from Genie's arms.

"How you doing, baby brother," she said to Jon, coming to sit next to him.

"Alive, but other than that, I don't think I've ever felt worse."

Genie turned around in the chair, looking around the room, searching.

"Don't worry," Jake said. "She's not here. Your brother told her how much you two hated her and pretty much drove her away." Jake gave her back the baby. "I have to leave. Where are your keys?"

Jon pointed to the small cabinet. Jake pulled out the drawer, took the keys, then slammed it shut. "Later," he said, his bile rising.

As soon as Jake was gone, Genie hissed at her brother. "You told him that?"

"Well, yeah. I was drunk. Told him Mom was probably turning over in her grave." A slight smile started on Jon's face. "Actually, I can't say I regret that."

"Idiot! What? You think Mom's gonna come back and say, 'Oh, Jake, I was just kidding. I'm not really dead. Let's go to the movies tonight."

"What are you talking about, Genie. Have you been drinking?"

"No! Just because you keep messing up your own life, why do you think you have to ruin his? Yes, I'm pissed that he's dating less than a year after she passed, but this is when Mary came back to check on her mother. It's not as if she was hanging around, waiting for Mom to die."

"But what about us?"

"What about us? We're adults. Shit," she covered the baby's ears and repeated herself, "Shit, you have your own life and I have mine. What? You want to go back to high school and be on the baseball team, reliving zits, raging hormones, and final exams? Be a kid again? We had our chance to learn from Dad. We'll always have him as an

58

example, but that doesn't mean he has to be celibate and eat dinner alone every night, sleep by himself. He deserves a companion as much as we do. Shoot," she uncovered the fussy baby's ears, "he has more right than we do. He has a lot less time left on this earth. That is, unless a drunk driver comes our way…"

"All right, all right. I get it. Dad already beat me over the head with the don't drink and drive manual."

"Yeah, but are you going to pay attention? You know as well as I do, as soon as they fire you, you'll want to drown your sorrows in the suds of the Rockies."

"From what Dad was saying, this time I'll have to spend time in jail. I think they have to make sure my legs are working right first, though."

"I wouldn't count on it. They may let you out on bail until your trial date, but I wouldn't count on Dad to kick in a nickel. I would if I could, but you know my financial situation. I barely have enough for rent and diapers."

"About the other thing…" Jon said, wincing as he tried to sit up straighter.

Genie pulled the pillow out from behind him, fluffed it, and repositioned it for him. "What other thing?"

"Mary," he said and rolled his eyes.

"Lots of luck there. If you have any money, why don't you give me some before the lawyer gets it all? I'll send her roses."

"But they're over ten bucks a dozen delivered! I know because I've sent at least three dozen to Chrissy. Didn't work, though."

"You messed up that relationship too much for the rose cure.

Mary's not your girlfriend but you still owe her a major 'I'm sorry.' Give a dozen yellow roses a try. Maybe it's not too late."

"Yellow? I thought red roses…"

"You forgot. I used to work at a florist. Yellow roses are for a friend you're apologizing to. Red is for lovers."

"Ew. Yeah, my wallet's in the cabinet. Get twenty bucks. If the first dozen doesn't cut it, maybe a second one will."

***

"Thanks for the ride, Pastor. Glad I caught you."

"Anytime. I'll drop in and see Jon when I'm doing my rounds tomorrow. If he has a broken leg, I'll have a captive audience."

"Best way to get him to listen," Jake said. "I'll see you Sunday."

It was now mid-morning and the sun shone bright, promising another hot day. Jake got in the Jeep, then realized it stank like stale beer. He looked behind the seat and saw several bags of fast-food trash and several empty beer cans. "Piggy kid," he said, then went in the house for a trash bag and a broom.

Big items purged, he drove the Jeep onto the lawn. Using the garden hose, he sprayed it out, saving the soap and scrubbing until after he'd removed the first two layers of stink. "Well, I guess it's a good thing you got the cheap version, Jon. Rubber mats are easier to hose down than carpet."

As he was drying off the red utility vehicle, he realized he was claiming it, cleaning it up for his own use. "Might as well. It'll be years before he can drive again. Idiot."

By the time he was waxing it, it dawned on him he was just

eating up time. Mary had been back in his life less than two weeks. Not having her near, or knowing she would be coming over soon, had left a familiar void. She wasn't dead but gone just the same. He couldn't let Jon's harsh words keep her away forever. He had to do something. He pulled his wallet out of his hip pocket and took out the little Christmas wish tag he had found three days earlier, meaning to show it to Mary at the picnic. 'My wish is for us to be together forever. Love, Mary.'

He quickly buffed out the coat of wax he'd put on the hood and called the job done. "I don't care if it's going to be a hundred and five today, I'm baking cookies."

Jake cleaned up, put on one of Ellen's old aprons, and grabbed the cookbook. "Jam thumbprint cookies and snickerdoodles, coming up."

Two hours and twenty degrees hotter later, he was done. "Now, for the perfect platter and note." He washed and dried his hands for the fifteenth time and started composing. "'How do I love thee...' Nah, too trite. 'If the night has a thousand eyes...' Nope, sounds like a pop song."

He pulled out his wallet again and looked at the note. "'My wish is for us to be together forever. Love, Jake.' It worked for me for nearly four years. Here's hoping a Christmas wish still works in June."

Note written and cookies finished, it was time for him to clean up. A tepid shower helped him cool off and calm down. "I feel like a kid again, ready to ask her out to the prom. Geez."

Looking in the mirror, he noticed how many gray hairs he had.

"Don't knock 'em. Twenty years from now, you'll be looking back on this day and remembering how 'old' you thought you were. You're a young bullock, Jake Johnson. You and Mary have at least thirty years ahead of you. And if she turns you down today, you can try again tomorrow. And the next day. And the next day." He sighed. "Here's hoping she sees reason and knows I won't give up on us. We were meant to be and that's that."

***

An hour later, Jake was at Mrs. Decker's front door, a plate of Christmas cookies in hand, a bead of nervous sweat on his upper lip. He quickly wiped it away, then rang the doorbell.

Mary answered the door, then looked behind him. "Where's the truck?" she asked.

"Hello to you, too," Jake said with a chuckle of insecurity. "I mean... I don't have it. It's a long story. Sort of. I brought you an apology gift. I should never have let you leave."

"Cookies?" she asked, sniffing them. "These don't look like store bought. Did you bake cookies in this heat, Jake Johnson?"

Jake grinned and shrugged, offering her the sweets. "You can keep the plate if you'd like, too. I mean, I have other ones. I guess you can't tell, but these are Christmas cookies. And see, I put my Christmas wish on it for you."

"Come in and sit down," Mary said, opening the door the rest of the way. "Mom, would you like some cookies and milk? Jake baked us a treat."

Mrs. Decker frowned at Jake, then saw his discomfort and grinned. "Just messing with you, Jake, seeing if I still got it. Yup, I do. Come and sit with me. It's about time I spoiled my supper with something not good for me."

Mary set the cookies on the table, then grabbed the fancy glasses and dessert plates from the china cabinet. He looked up at her, smiled, then saw her look to the bouquet of yellow roses in the center of the table.

"Those are beautiful," he said. "Don't tell me you already have another admirer."

"Read the tag," Mary said, then left to get the milk.

"'I am so sorry. Please forgive me. And do not be mad at Dad. He loves you. Jon.'" Jake turned the card over and saw the florist's name. "When did these come?"

"About an hour ago. Genie delivered them. She said she was sorry for being rude to me, but that when Jon said we hated you, it was the beer talking, and he certainly had no right to speak for her."

"Did she tell you he wrecked my truck?"

"He did? No. She said due to extenuating circumstances, he asked her to order the flowers for him. After he told her what he had said, she decided it would be a good idea to deliver them herself so she could apologize for her own rude behavior. Plus, the money she'd save could be put toward more flowers. There are a dozen and a half here, plus the Baby's Breath."

"Do I have to wait until you two stop talking or can I have my snack now?" Mrs. Decker asked, holding her plate in one hand, her glass out with the other.

Mary took the glass and filled it while Jake unwrapped the plastic wrap. "The note's just for you, Mary, but the cookies are to share."

"Ah, snickerdoodles, my favorite. But you forgot the red sprinkles."

"I didn't have anyone there to make them for me. Do you want to help next time?"

"Can we wait until a cool day? I still have a watermelon to carve into a basket of melon balls. That won't heat up the kitchen."

"Does that mean we're back where we're supposed to be?" Jake asked.

"Lord, I hope so," Mrs. Decker said. "She's been crying and moping ever since she got back here yesterday. You two were meant to be together. Period. Anyone who ever saw you two would know it, too. Unless he was blind drunk."

"Oh, speaking of blind drunk…" Jake said. "Jon flipped my truck into a ditch and totaled it. He got busted with a third DUI. He's going to be spending some time in jail. Here's hoping they have some sobriety classes. At least he can detox away from booze."

"Oh, my Lord. Is he all right?" Mary asked.

"Broken leg, a few stitches, a couple black eyes, and a broken nose. He'll be fine. That is, if he realizes he's supposed to be stronger and smarter than a can of beer. When he starts listening to the liquor talk, he's in trouble."

Chapter 8: Second Chances

December 25, 1976

"Merry Christmas and happy six-month anniversary," Jake said, handing Mary a box.

"I thought we weren't going to get each other 'stuff' this year."

"As I remember it, we weren't going to *buy* each other stuff," Jake said. "I made this."

Mary unwrapped the box and brought out a carved wooden platter with a dozen wooden 'cookies.' She picked one up. "Pine jam thumbprints and..." She picked up another one. "Birch snickerdoodles?"

"Alder," Jake said, "but close enough. What time is everyone coming over?"

Mary held out a package to him. "Open mine first and I'll tell you."

Jake removed the reclaimed Christmas wrapping paper and blinked back tears. "It's beautiful. How'd you do it?"

Mary took the plaque from him and pointed out the details. "First, I know my way around power tools, too, but you know that. I made a simple plaque, had the office supply store make a photocopy of the old photograph, then used a little goop and white glue, and *Voila!* The ink from the copied photo transferred onto the wood. It's a little irregular the way it came off, but I think it adds to the vintage charm. Oh, and of course I had to carve and burn the edges a little to give it a rustic Arizona look."

"Pioneer stock, for sure. I don't remember when they took this picture. I mean, I was only three years old, but I do remember seeing the original on the wall for years. How'd you get it away from the heritage house?"

"Well, I know a wonderful newlywed couple who happen to volunteer at the Fort Huachuca Museum. They did a little display swapping with Bisbee. The copying didn't harm the original. Now we have our own version for the living room."

Knock, knock, knock.

"Ah, and here they are," Jake said. He opened the door and Scooter and Linda came in, their adopted twin sons rushing past them to the box of oversized building blocks.

"You'd think they were two instead of eight," Linda said.

"What they can do with modeling clay is amazing," Scooter said. "And here the agency said they were hard to place. First time we saw them, we knew they belonged in our hearts and lives."

"Hey, Dad. Can we make some like these, too? Uncle Jake said they're real easy to make out of scraps," the dark-skinned boy said.

"Maybe you and Uncle Jake can work something out. You and your brother can trade yard work or chores for blocks," Scooter said.

"Sounds good to me," Jake said.

Honk, honk!

"That's either Genie or Jon," Mary said.

"We'll go help them in," the boys said, then stood up.

"Go ahead," Linda said. "Remember your manners."

"Yes, Mom."

"It's both of them," Jake told Mary. "All five of them are carpooling."

"Five?" Linda asked.

"Oh, I guess you didn't know. The x-ray tech at the hospital took a shine to Genie and young Jacob. They've been dating since Jon had to come back to have that screw in his leg removed."

"That makes four including Jon," Linda said.

"And Jon stopped sending roses and started writing sincere letters to Chrissy, asking for another chance, swearing off alcohol, even one to celebrate their wedding."

"They're married?" Scooter asked.

"Nope. But he said if she'd marry him, he'd have to toast her with apple juice. Nothing, even being wed to her, was worth drinking again. He'd learned his lesson."

"It's a good thing no one but him was hurt in that last DUI," Scooter said. "I'd say there was a bit of Divine intervention getting him off with only four months in jail."

"Six months with time off for good behavior," Jake said, "but who's counting. Your impassioned speech before the judge made a big difference. I'm glad Jon's stood by his word. Look at him now."

Scooter came to the plexiglass-paned door and watched Jon lifting young Leroy – or was that Elroy? – up in the air, the twin brother loaded with bags of gifts and a big stuffed lion. "I never thought I'd be so rich in friends and family."

"New and old, by blood or by choice," Jake said, his hand on his friend's shoulder. "All priceless."

An hour later, the gathering of family and friends sat at the fully extended table loaded with food, forks, and elbows. "Here's to great friends and family…" Jake said, his cup of cider raised in a toast.

"And second chances, both in love and health," Jon said, glass up.

"And first chances, too," Genie's boyfriend added, giving her a squeeze with one hand, the other toasting with the group.

"Here, here!" Scooter said. "Merry Christmas to all, and to all a good life!"

The End

THANK YOU!

Thank you for reading my stand-alone novella, *A Plate of Christmas Cookies.* The story was sparked by a moment in time I witnessed. Thirty-five years after returning home from Iwo Jima, 'Jake' met his former high school sweetheart again. 'Mary' really did have curlers in her hair that evening, too. They married and lived happily ever after.

Other Books by Dani Haviland

ARLIE UNDERCOVER (romantic suspense based in Alaska and Arizona)

A Stingray Christmas: (Book One) Anchorage detective on medical leave travels from Alaska to Arizona to see for the first time the son he'd fathered as an anonymous sperm donor. Great and rotten surprises await the cop with the smartest smartphone around.

The Biggest Heart Ever: (Book Two) When would Arlie learn that trying to do everything by himself could be deadly—and make Charlene a widow before they were married?

Always a Bigger Fish: (Book Three) Back in Alaska, Arlie finds out he's a target. Will vacationing detective Billy Burke (from THE FAIRIES SAGA) have information to help nab the scalper?

How to Fix a Broken Life: (Book Four) When Arlie's very pregnant wife is kidnapped by pseudo terrorists, will he be the one to rescue her or will a surprise hero come in to save the day?

Because You Said So: (Book Five) Something's amiss at the Port of Anchorage. Will Arlie be able to solve it and still be back in time to wear the Santa suit?

Heaven and Heartbreak (Book Six) Sharing her child with a gay father and his lover was the easy part. Finding a woman for herself seemed impossible.

THAT TWIN THING SERIES (romantic suspense series)

The Midwife's Son: The midwife refused her selfish patient's request to smother the scrawny twin and instead took him home to bring up as her own. Years later, will the two young men wind up in each other's lives despite the midwife's efforts to keep them apart?

Phoenix I'm Not: Will the billionaire's spoiled son be resurrected from the ashes of his former life of drugs and mayhem by love or be tortured and eliminated by the assassin sent by his mother?

Lost and Found Family: Separated at birth, these twins find they have more than genetics in common: they're both the target of killers who are willing to risk everything to take them out.

Peter Elph: A supplement to the story of Lost and Found Family, this short story is about a member of the Wagner family back in 1886 Tombstone, Arizona.

That Twin Thing: The Complete Collection: All four books in one place.

THE FAIRIES SAGA SERIES (historical fiction/time travel, listed in order with novellas):

Kibbles and Bits: FREE ebook: Sample the first stories in the series before you buy. The Fairies Saga stories. Find out how the first five books got their crazy names, too.

Naked in the Winter Wind: (Book One) How does an older woman wind up as a young hottie in Revolutionary War era North Carolina? First book in the time travel series.

Ha'Penny Jenny: (Book Two) More about the naïve and psychic young girl who was adopted into a time traveling family. Will her past catch up to her?

Aye, I am a Fairy: (Book Three) Young British lord finds himself entwined with a time traveling family and must decide if he should go back in time, too. Second book in the series.

Dances Naked: (Book Four) Directionally challenged time traveler is rescued by Cherokee in 18th century. What must he do before the chief will show him to The Trees, the portal through time?

Chasing Christmas: (Book Five) A young Cherokee is rescued from an abusive man and changes the lives of many in this 18th century America family.

The Great Big Fairy: (Book Six) Very tall Benji grew up in the 20th century but was born in the 18th. When he finds a way to return to his grandparents in the distant past, he goes for it. Once there, he realizes he can't stay, but must return to the future.

Little Bear and the Ladies: (Book Seven) What's a bachelor trapper to do with all the females he rescues from the Hessian mercenaries? He'd better hurry and figure something!

Little Drummer Boy: (Book Eight) Young Scout works to earn money for a home in post-Revolutionary War America but runs up against prejudices and snowstorms.

Never Too Young: (Book Nine) Scout and Ha'Penny Jenny have grown up, but will they be able to spend their life together, or will the past and ruffians get in their way?

Time in a Little Blue Bottle: (Book Ten) Elvis, Mark Twain, and the prime vampire are racing to get the bottle of Fountain of Youth water before sweet Bella and the youthful pickpocket. So why are time travelers Marty Melbourne and Master Simon interested?

Kidnapped! (Book Eleven) The Scottish police officer would do anything to get his wife back...even trust the mysterious letter sent to him from his ancestor, a convict on The First Fleet into Australia!

Big Mac: (Book Twelve) Fate and science said they should never have met but after that first touch, he knew he'd stay with her forever. Would the sudden appearance of the father he never knew be their doom – and the start of a pandemic?

CONTEMPORARY NOVELLAS – BENJI, THE LOST YEARS

Pool Boy Wanted: No Experience Preferred: (rather racy) Young Benji has been a hostage and slave, but life gets worse when an older woman decides she wants him as her own.

Luke the Unexpected: Love of classic motorcycles brought them together, but Luke and Holly have other challenges to face. Find out how their friend Benji got his stripes here.

STAND ALONE NOVELLAS (contemporary romances)

Kit Kringle: An Alaskan Tale: Kay moved to Alaska for the wrong reasons, then decided to stay and start her own business. What she hadn't planned on were prejudices and falling in love.

Be My Angel: Wyatt's dream to help save the wild mustangs began with the purchase of a rundown ranch in western Oregon. What he hadn't anticipated was being mesmerized by a sassy woman in a wheelchair.

Three Are One: The post chaplain tried to help the young widow adjust, but would his feelings for her and the search for his lost sister cause problems?

One Arctic Summer: That unforgettable summer of 1994 in Barrow, Alaska, and the touch she never forgot…If she goes back, will he remember her?

The Polar Xpress: Will the California chiropractor get a first chance at romance with the owner of Second Chance Kennels when he is stranded in Alaska?

Too Fast For You: Ten years after Little League, two talented professional baseball players wind up on the same minor league team. Will she remember him? And will their friendship be ruined if she does?

TRIPLETS: THREE *AREN'T* ONE *(A potpourri of literary styles, all with strong characters)*

The Set Up: Grace's story. A gritty women's fiction of how it all began.

Diamonds Aren't for Everyone: Vickie's story. A billionaire romance.

That Magic Touch: Ria's story. A medical romance

How Love Grows: Tori's story. A romantic-comedy.

They Call Me Sherlock: Silas's story. A romantic-comedy with a touch of time travel.

About the Author

Author Dani Haviland started writing late in life and has been making up for lost time with a flood of works from sports, gritty tales, time travel, and Sweet and Sassy romances to Unforgettable romantic suspense, Cute But Crazy rom-coms, and cozy mystery stories – with some Shorts thrown in to round out the reading experience.

Dani is also the owner of *Chill Out! Books*, one of the publishers for *The Authors' Billboard*. Follow her on Amazon (http://bit.ly/dhAuthor) and BookBub (https://www.bookbub.com/authors/dani-haviland) to make sure you get her latest stories.

Contact information:

Website: www.danihaviland.com

Email: dani@danihaviland.com

Twitter: @dani_haviland, @gr8authors

I love to hear from readers!

Sign up for my newsletter to get the latest information on new releases, free stuff, and contests at: http://bit.ly/2DHnews

Awesome readers group!

I have a Facebook Page for folks who are interested in early excerpts and insights into my latest books and box sets. I'd appreciate a like on the page. Drop in and see if I've remembered to add photos and excerpts of my works in process. Dani Haviland & Friends Readers Group (https://www.facebook.com/ChillOutDani)

www.ingramcontent.com/pod-product-compliance
Lightning Source LLC
Chambersburg PA
CBHW071236170626

46809CB00008BA/3079